The WISH LIBRARY

The Vanishing Friend

The WISH LIBRARY

The Vanishing Friend

Christine Evans

illustrated by Patrick Corrigan

ALBERT WHITMAN & COMPANY
CHICAGO, ILLINOIS

To Vicky & Faith; my writing wishes
came true because of you!—CE

To Edie and George—PC

Library of Congress Cataloging-in-Publication
data is on file with the publisher.

Text copyright © 2023 by Christine Evans
Illustrations copyright © 2023 by Albert Whitman & Company
Illustrations by Patrick Corrigan
First published in the United States of America in 2023
by Albert Whitman & Company
ISBN 978-0-8075-8100-1 (hardcover)
ISBN 978-0-8075-8101-8 (ebook)

Printed in the United States of America
10 9 8 7 6 5 4 3 2 1 LB 28 27 26 25 24 23

Design by Erin McMahon

For more information about Albert Whitman & Company,
visit our website at www.albertwhitman.com.

Contents

CHAPTER 1

Redwood Rescue Farm

Luca Flores and Raven Rose waved as their parents drove away. Then they looked at each other and high-fived.

"This is going to be the best week ever!" said Luca.

"No little sisters, no parents, and..." Raven lowered her voice to a whisper. "No magic wishes!"

Raven and Luca had gotten lots of experience with magic ever since they'd discovered the entrance to a magical Wish Library on the grounds of their school. Within the library, they could check out wishes for almost anything they wanted, just like checking out books from a regular library.

But as fun as it was to check out the wishes, they didn't always go as planned. During Raven and Luca's last visit, a unicorn had escaped, and the Librarian had needed their help to recover it—or else she would have been in big trouble with Wish Library HQ.

Raven was glad there would be no magical mishaps to worry about at Redwood Rescue Farm. Just horses, pigs, chickens, and lots of fun. She'd been looking forward to this camp for months.

"Okay, campers!" said a camp leader through a megaphone. "Welcome to Redwood Rescue Farm! Let's get you settled into your cabins!"

One by one, the camp leader called out names. Each cabin was named after a different type of animal the rescue farm took in.

"Luca Flores, you're a Barn Owl!" the camp leader called.

Luca waved bye to Raven and went to join his cabinmates. He immediately started talking to the other boys. Raven watched him laughing, jealous for a moment at how easily he made new friends.

"Raven Rose, you're part of the Rabbits!" the camp leader said.

Raven joined her group and followed them toward the cabins. She clutched her bag. At home,

she shared a room with her sister, Izzy. She'd never spent a night away from her family before.

On the outside of the girls' cabin was a mural of rabbits playing. Inside, the cabin had six beds made neatly with colorful quilts. Next to each bed was a chest of drawers for their belongings. The campers would be staying for a full week, so Raven was happy to have a place to put her things.

"Hi, Rabbits! I'm Jess," Raven's cabin leader said as she entered. She was dressed in shorts, boots, and a Redwood Rescue Farm shirt. Her hair was neatly tied back in a pony-tail. "Unpack your things and get settled. I'll see you in twenty minutes for our farm tour. Don't forget to wear boots and your name tags!"

Raven met the five other girls in her cabin: Anna, Kiora, Sally, Freya, and Naomi. She was glad they had name tags, as she had already forgotten all the names the camp leader had announced. When everyone was ready, the campers pulled on their boots and met Jess outside their cabin. Raven smiled at her new friends as they waited to find out what they would be doing first.

"Okay, Rabbits," Jess said. "We're going to join the Barn Owls to meet some of the animals and complete your first camp chore. Let's go!"

Jess led the way down a short dirt path to a cabin that looked just like the one Raven was staying in, except it had a Barn Owl mural on one side. Redwood trees towered over the cabins and kept them shaded. Raven shivered a little. She wished

she'd put on a sweater.

The Barn Owl leader was named Justin, and he was checking off names from his clipboard. He wore jeans and the same camp shirt as Jess. "Luca, Will, Jasper, Ellis, Austin, and Andy."

With everyone accounted for, Jess and Justin led the twelve kids down a path out of the shade of the giant trees. The sun beamed into the farmyard. There were horse stables, a chicken coop, goats,

sheep, and pigs.

Luca and Raven fell into step next to each other. "How are your cabinmates?" Luca asked.

"They seem nice," said Raven. "Hopefully no one snores! How about yours?"

"Same," he said. "Jasper brought chocolate chip cookies, so he's my new best friend."

"Hey!" said Raven, nudging Luca with her elbow.

He laughed. "Only joking! But he is nervous about not knowing anyone here so I told him we'd be his friends."

Raven and Luca had been best friends ever since Luca had helped Raven return her very first wish to the Wish Library. But they both knew what it was like to be lonely. When Luca first moved to Lincoln, he hadn't known anyone, and Raven's best friend had just moved away.

The group stopped at a pen full of pigs. Jess explained that all the animals at the farm had been rescued from places that couldn't look after them anymore. The campers would be learning how to clean Buttercup and her piglets' pen out tomorrow. But today they were going to work in the hen coop collecting eggs.

Raven waved at the piglets. Her dad was a zookeeper at Lincoln Zoo, and she loved animals too. She couldn't wait to play with the piglets, snuggle the goats, and make new friends.

Some of the campers held their noses at the smell of the pig poop. "Everyone takes part in the chores at farm camp," said Jess. "It's how we keep everything running smoothly and keep the animals healthy."

Luca couldn't wait to get to know the animals. He'd never had a pet, and he hoped his mom would consider one if he proved he could look after farm animals this week.

"Get into groups, and we'll pass out the egg-collecting baskets," said Justin.

Raven and Luca gathered chicken eggs with Jasper from the Barn Owl cabin. "They're all

different colors!" said Jasper. "Not like the boring brown ones from the store."

"And this one has a feather stuck to it," Raven said, adding an egg to their basket. She had never held a fresh egg before. It was still warm.

The group finished collecting eggs. Then Justin led the campers to the kitchen to drop the eggs off.

"This is Chef Amanda," Justin explained. "She

uses produce from the farm to make our meals."

Chef Amanda waved at everyone as she prepared salad leaves. Luca spotted bowls of fresh strawberries on the counter. Everything looked delicious.

"Now let's meet more animals," said Jess. She led the way back into the farmyard. "Here are our goats. The adults were all rescued together, and the kids were born just a couple of months ago."

Raven grinned as the baby goats skipped and climbed on rocks in the pen.

"And over in the stables we have our beautiful horses," said Justin. "Like all our animals, they are rescues too, but they're healthy and thriving now."

"In fact, they're ready to take you all for a gentle ride through the redwoods," said Jess.

Justin and Jess helped the kids put on helmets and mount their horses. Raven's was brown and named May, and Luca's gray horse was called Sky.

"What's your horse's name?" Raven asked Jasper.

"Um, Nacho, I think," Jasper said. He clutched his reins tightly and looked terrified.

"Are you okay?" asked Luca.

"I've never been this close to a horse before," Jasper said. "And I've never even been to a farm."

"I haven't ridden a horse either," said Raven.

"But don't worry. They know what to do."

Sure enough, once they were started, the horses walked nose to tail through the forest. Luca led the way on Sky, followed by Raven on May and Jasper on Nacho.

Suddenly, Sky stopped, and May stepped away.

"What happened?" asked Luca, looking back at Raven. "Did I do something wrong?"

Raven shrugged.

Jasper pointed to the ground, where Sky had left a pile of poop.

"Ewww!" the three said together, laughing.

Later, after dinner in the barn, the campers helped gather wood and pine needles. Then the leaders started a campfire.

"Tonight we're going to learn camp songs and make s'mores," said Jess. It was everything Raven and Luca had been looking forward to.

"We're at farm camp," chanted Jess.

"We're at farm camp," repeated all the kids.

"Redwood Rescue Camp," Jess called.

"Redwood Rescue Camp," they called back.

"We're here to help animals."

"We're here to help animals."

"And we're gonna make friends!"

Raven and Luca smiled at Jasper as they repeated, "We're gonna make friends!"

At the end of the song, Justin handed out skewers and marshmallows.

"Yum!" Luca looked up at the stars. "I wish this day could last forever."

"Me too!" said Jasper. He sandwiched his marsh-mallow with a square of chocolate between two crackers to make his s'more.

"Be careful making wishes!" Raven whispered to Luca. But secretly she wished the same as Luca. It had been an amazing day.

"It's okay, we're miles away from the Wish Library," Luca whispered back.

"We're miles away from *our* Wish Library," said Raven. "But there could be another branch here somewhere."

Raven looked at Jasper to make sure he hadn't heard them, but he was busy making a second s'more.

Luca thought Raven worried too much. And who needed wishes when camp was everything they'd hoped for?

CHAPTER 2

Oink!

The next morning, a rooster crowed at six o'clock and woke all the campers. Raven groaned and put a pillow over her head. Farm days started early! But she was excited to find out what they would be doing for the day.

"Rise and shine, Rabbits!" said Jess. "After breakfast it's your turn to clean out the animal pens!"

Raven groaned again. If she could have made a wish right then it would have been for all the animals' pens to get magically cleaned. She preferred riding horses and seeing the animals, not cleaning up after them.

———

"This is even more disgusting than your horse pooping in front of me!" Raven said, shoveling dirty straw into a wheelbarrow.

The Rabbits and Barn Owls had been split up to clean out different animal pens. Raven and Luca were assigned to the goats.

"You need one of these," said Luca pointing to a clothespin on his nose. It made his voice sound funny. "Austin handed them out this morning to keep the smells out."

Raven wished someone in her cabin had thought of something to block the stink. Jasper waved from the next pen as he and Anna cleaned the pigpen. He had a clothespin on his nose too.

Despite the smell, Raven kept working until they had shoveled out all the old bedding and laid fresh, clean straw for the goats.

"Good job, Raven and Luca!" Justin said. "Now that you've finished the hard part, you can feed the goats and their kids."

Luca and Raven poured goat feed into the feeding troughs. The goats nudged Raven and Luca out of the way so they could get to their food.

Raven giggled. "They're so funny!" Even when one kid started chewing her shirt sleeve instead of its food, she laughed. Cleaning out the goat pen was worthwhile if it meant she could spend time with the animals after.

Jess handed Raven a brush so she could groom the goats. "They love being groomed almost as much as they love food," she said.

In the next pen, Jasper turned around with a shovel full of dirty bedding to say something to Raven and Luca. But he didn't see Buttercup, the mama pig, right behind him. As he turned, he tripped over her and fell headfirst into a mound of pig mud! SPLAT!

Jasper pushed himself up slowly. SQUELCH! He was covered from head to toe in brown, sticky mud. Buttercup oinked at Jasper as if to say "Watch where you're going!"

Kiora was in the next pen feeding the chickens. "Ewww!" she called out. "You stink like a pig, Jasper! Oink, oink!"

Anna bent over laughing and pointed at Jasper. "Oink, oink!" she chanted.

As more of the campers joined in the chanting, Jasper ran out of the pigpen.

"Are you okay?" Luca called out.

Jasper ran toward the pond by the animal pens. Quacking ducks scattered as he made his way toward the water. But before he could get close enough to wash off the mud, Jasper slipped again. When he stood up, he was covered in leaves and sticks.

"Aaaaargh!" shouted Anna. "It's a swamp monster! Run for your lives!" Now, all the other Rabbits and Barn Owls were laughing.

Jasper wasn't laughing along, Luca realized. "I think we should help him," he said to Raven.

They climbed out of the goat pen and ran to help Jasper. But before they could reach him, he raced into the redwood forest.

Luca and Raven chased after Jasper, following the trail they'd ridden the day before.

"Where did he go?" said Raven.

Luca stopped in the middle of the trail and held his hand up. "Did you hear that?"

"No," Raven looked around. "What?"

"I heard someone talking," Luca said. "This way!" Luca led the way deeper into the trees.

This tree is 200+ years old

They called out for Jasper over and over. But there was no sign of him. The two friends stood under a gigantic redwood tree marked with a sign. They looked around for a clue about where Jasper had gone. But he had vanished.

"We need to tell Justin and Jess!" said Raven. A missing camper was serious. She hoped Jasper was okay.

Raven and Luca ran as fast as they could back to camp.

At the pens, everyone was carrying on with their jobs as if nothing had happened. No one was laughing or oinking. Jess and Justin were helping Anna with the pigs.

"As you haven't got a partner, we'll give you a hand," said Jess to Anna.

Raven and Luca looked at each other, confused.

"Anna has a partner!" Luca said to Jess. "Jasper! He just ran into the woods covered in..."

Suddenly, Luca stopped talking. He'd forgotten what he was going to say.

"Who?" said Justin. He showed Raven and Luca his clipboard. "We don't have a Jasper here this week."

Raven and Luca looked at the clipboard. There were only five boys' names listed in the Barn Owl cabin. None of them were Jasper.

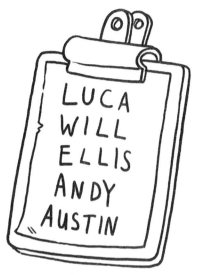

LUCA
WILL
ELLIS
ANDY
AUSTIN

"Where did you two go?" asked Jess. "You still have goats to groom."

Raven and Luca couldn't remember what they had been talking about. Or why they had gone into the woods. There must have been a reason, but they had no memory of it. Which was weird.

Raven and Luca shrugged and climbed back into the pen to finish brushing the goats. *Whatever it was,* Raven thought, *it couldn't have been* that *important. Could it?*

CHAPTER 3

Chicken Chaos

"The food here is amazing," said Luca, eagerly eating his egg salad sandwich. "Freshly laid eggs taste so good!" Even the salad tasted better than normal, as it had been harvested that morning by kids from one of the other cabins.

Raven thought back to the morning. Playing with the goats had been the highlight of the week so far. But something was bothering her. She had a slightly sick feeling, like she'd forgotten something important. *Maybe it's something planned for later,* she thought.

"What are we doing this afternoon?" she asked.

Luca looked at the schedule posted on the barn wall. "A scavenger hunt!" he said.

"Cool!" said Raven. She looked at the schedule too. They had another campfire later in the evening. The rest of the schedule contained chores, arts and crafts, more trail rides, and finally a barn dance party at the end of the week.

Raven tried to shake off her worry. *It must just be the chores,* she thought.

After lunch, Jess and Justin handed out lists of items the kids would need to find on their scavenger hunt.

"The first team back here with all the items wins a day free from chores!" said Justin. "You can go anywhere on the farm or the redwood forest trails."

Luca and Raven looked at each other.

"Let's win this!" said Luca, high-fiving Raven.

"What's on the list?" Raven asked.

Luca read out the items they had to find:

SOMETHING ROUND
SOMETHING SPIKY
SOMETHING SOFT
SOMETHING LONG
SOMETHING TINY
SOMETHING GREEN
SOMETHING OLD

"Wow, that's a lot," said Raven. "Where should we start?" They looked around the farm. Other campers were already hunting for objects.

"Let's go into the forest first," said Luca. "We can definitely get something green there."

Under the shade of the redwood trees, Luca found a fallen branch. "Something green!" he said.

"Or something old!" said Raven, standing at a sign beneath one of the gigantic trees. "This sign says this redwood is more than two hundred years old." Something was strangely familiar about the tree. Raven felt like she'd seen the sign before.

"Cool!" said Luca. He opened his mouth to say something else but stopped when he heard a twig snap behind him.  He turned around, but there was no one there. Then he thought he heard footsteps running away from them.

"Hello?" he called out.

"What's wrong?" asked Raven.

"I was sure I heard someone," said Luca. "But maybe I imagined it." Luca felt strange. Like this very same thing had happened to him before. His mom called it déjà vu when it happened to her sometimes.

"Umm, do they have bears here?" asked Raven,

looking around. She did not want to meet a bear.

"No, they don't live here," said Luca. At least, he was pretty sure they didn't. But he thought maybe they should leave just in case. "Let's go back to the farm to find more items so we can win!"

"What have we got so far?" asked Raven. Luca read the list with each item they'd found.

Something round: a stone

Something spiky: a pine cone

Something long: a stick

Something tiny: an acorn

Something green: a leaf

Something old: a redwood branch

"We just need something soft!" said Raven. She pointed at the chicken coop. "I have an idea!"

She led Luca to the chicken coop so they could look for a feather. "Hang on," she said, looking around. "Where are the chickens?"

Luca pointed at the coop gate, which was swinging open. "Someone left the gate open."

Just then a shriek came from the Barn Owl cabin. "Help!" yelled Austin, running out.

Raven and Luca ran to him. "What's wrong?" they asked.

"Come see for yourselves!" said Austin.

Raven and Luca ran into the cabin. In each of the six beds in the Barn Owl cabin, there was a chicken, and under each chicken was an egg.

Luca chased the one in his bed out the door. The other four boys did the same. One chicken was left in an unoccupied bed in the Barn Owl cabin. Luca

chased it out. *That's weird,* he thought. *I thought we had a full cabin when we arrived.*

But he must have been muddled up. There had definitely only been five boys on Justin's list earlier. Something felt blurry in Luca's brain, like he'd forgotten something important. But he shook his head and joined the rest of the campers.

CHAPTER 4

Missing

After Justin and Jess helped the kids secure the chickens in the chicken coop, they called a camp meeting.

"Does anyone know how the chickens got into the cabin?" asked Jess.

"Maybe someone left the coop open?" said Austin.

"I checked it this morning after we cleaned all the pens," said Justin. "It was closed then."

No one admitted to letting the chickens out.

"Okay," said Jess. "Let's make sure it doesn't happen again. All the animal pens must be kept shut. We have lots of wild animals that live in the forest. Sometimes mountain lions make their way down here."

Raven's eyes widened. Lions?! She had no idea they lived here. *Maybe that's what we heard in the forest,* she thought.

"Who won the scavenger hunt?" asked Austin.

"Let's find out!" said Jess. "Did anyone find all the items on the list?"

Sally and Freya put their arms in the air.

Raven groaned. She and Luca had forgotten about the last item. She had really wanted to win and not have to do any chores.

"Congratulations, Sally and Freya!" said Justin. "Now, it's almost dinnertime. Everyone should go clean up, and we'll see you in the barn in thirty minutes."

Raven got changed into clean clothes for dinner. She had just started to brush her hair when she heard a scream from the bathroom. Raven knocked on the door, and Anna let her in.

"What's wrong?" asked Raven.

Anna was tugging at her hair with a brush. "My hairbrush!" she said. "It's stuck!"

Raven pulled at the brush, but it was firmly stuck in Anna's straight brown hair. Raven looked closer. "Someone put glue in it!" she said. "But it's okay. It's just craft glue. It'll come out if you wash it."

As Anna headed to the shower to get the sticky brush out of her hair, Raven wondered who would do such a thing. None of the Rabbits seemed like they would have played such a prank. Maybe one of the campers from a different cabin did it.

"Where's Teddy?" said Freya, throwing all the quilts from her bed on the floor.

"Who?" asked Raven.

"My bear. I've had him since I was born," said Freya. "I left him on my bed, and now I can't find him."

"I'll help you look," said Raven. She searched under all the beds and asked each camper to check their drawers, but there was no sign of Teddy. "Maybe he's outside?"

Raven and Freya looked around outside the cabin. They checked around the extinguished campfire and the pile of firewood. Then Freya cried and pointed up into a tree. Hanging in a branch was poor Teddy.

"I'll find Jess," Raven told Freya, who was crying harder now. "She can help get Teddy down."

While Jess helped Freya, Raven went back inside the cabin to finish getting ready for dinner. She was greeted by Sally, who showed her the

dragon book she'd been reading. "Someone tore out the last page," she said. "Now I don't know how it ends!"

Kiora showed Raven her journal. "That's not all!" she said. "Someone broke open the padlock! They might tell everyone my secrets!"

Raven wondered for a moment what Kiora's secrets were. But then Naomi came running inside.

She held what looked like a dirty rag in her hands. "My favorite sweatshirt was in the pigpen!"

Raven consoled her new friends. But she was relieved that none of her belongings had been messed with. *Who would do such a thing?* she wondered. *And how did they do it without being noticed?*

At dinner, Raven told Luca what had happened in the Rabbit cabin. "Everyone had something taken or tampered with except me," she said through a mouthful of food. That night's dinner was spaghetti and meatballs—one of her favorites.

"Same in our cabin!" said Luca. "Someone took out the laces from Austin's sneakers, Will's glasses were covered in slime, someone drew mustaches on Ellis's family photo, and Andy's water bottle was filled with salt water. But I haven't noticed any of my stuff being messed up…yet."

41

"Do you think someone from another cabin pranked everyone?" asked Raven.

"Maybe," said Luca, wrapping spaghetti around his fork. "But how did they do it without being spotted? And no one was missing during the scavenger hunt."

"It's like they were invisible," said Raven. She began to wonder if it was possible that someone had made a wish. Was there a Wish Library on Redwood Rescue Farm?

After dinner, Raven and Luca walked back to the cabins. At the door of the Rabbits' cabin, they heard clucking coming from inside. Raven peered in. There was once again a chicken in every bed. They looked very comfortable!

"Again?" Jess groaned, looking around the cabin. "We've never had this happen in the history of farm camp."

"Everyone was at dinner when it happened,"

said Raven. "No one could have let them out."

"Unless..." said Luca to Raven quietly. He thought back to when weird things had happened to them back in Lincoln. "Could someone have made a wish?"

"I've been thinking the same thing," whispered Raven. "It would explain everything that's happened."

"Let's get a flashlight," whispered Luca. "If there is a Wish Library here, I bet the entrance will be in the forest, just like the one to our library."

CHAPTER 5

The Wish Library

Raven led the way down the trail into the dark redwood forest, her flashlight shining ahead. Owls were hooting in the trees above, and something rustled in the undergrowth. Raven and Luca both knew they shouldn't be out in the forest on their own at night, especially after what Jess had said about mountain lions, but they needed to find out what was going on.

Raven stopped where they'd picked up the redwood branch earlier. The sign next to the giant tree still seemed so familiar.

"You thought you heard footsteps here during the scavenger hunt," said Raven. "Let's try making a wish and see if anything happens."

Luca thought about a suitable wish. He knew the entrance to a hidden Wish Library would only appear to someone who truly needed a wish to come true.

"I wish to go to the library!" said Luca.

They looked around. There was no magical coin to be seen. At home, they entered the Wish Library by tossing the coin down a wishing well.

Luca thought again. The wish needed to be something he truly needed. He really needed to know what was going on and how to fix it. "I wish to know who is pranking us!" he said.

This time, a gold coin appeared at Luca's feet. He picked it up. It was almost the same as the one that appeared at their Wish Library in Lincoln, but the picture of the Librarian looked different. That made sense, he supposed. Multiple Wish Libraries meant multiple librarians. He wondered what this librarian would be like. Theirs had a pet bearded dragon and wore roller skates. Plus, she was kind of scary at times.

"Look, there's the well!" Raven said, pointing behind Luca. The stone well looked exactly the same as the one in Lincoln.

"Here we go!" said Luca, throwing the coin into the well. And just like making a wish at the well in Lincoln, he fell down after the coin. But instead of free falling like usual, he found himself going head-first on a twisty slide.

"Ooof!" he said, landing on a soft cushion.

"Ow!" Raven said, crashing into him. She patted around for her glasses.

"Are you okay?" said a woman looking down at them. Raven put on her glasses, and the speaker came into focus. She was about five feet tall, and there was a small brown owl sitting on her shoulder.

"Who are you?" asked Raven, rubbing her head.

"I'm the Librarian, of course," said the woman.

"And who are you?"

"Raven Rose," said Raven. "And this is Luca Flores."

"Raven and Luca," said the Librarian. Her forehead creased. "Your names are very familiar…"

"Well, we do have a library in our town—" started Raven, but the Librarian interrupted her.

"Oh! You helped Prudence with her little unicorn issue. You are quite famous among us librarians, you know." The Librarian beamed and clapped her hands.

"Prudence?" said Luca, confused. He didn't know anyone named Prudence. Then he realized. "Oh…the Librarian!"

"Indeed, indeed! I'm so thrilled to meet you both," said the Librarian, shaking Luca's and Raven's hands. "Oh, where are my manners? Welcome to the Redwood Farm Wish Library. As you know, I'm the Librarian. And this is Elsie." The Librarian stroked the small owl.

Elsie hooted a hello.

Luca and Raven looked around. There was a weird old computer with levers and a dusty screen, just like the one in their library, and shelves full of test tubes and containers that each contained a wish. But unlike their library, redwood tree roots grew down from the ceiling.

"This redwood tree is as old as the Wish Library," said the Librarian, indicating the roots. "It was planted the day the library was founded over two hundred years ago. I have to keep rearranging the shelves as it grows."

The shelves in the Wish Library were arranged in neat rows, avoiding the roots. It was a much smaller library than the one in Lincoln, but the shelves reached up high above their heads.

"Elsie helps me fetch the wishes from the top shelves," said the Librarian. "She's a wonderful assistant."

Elsie hooted in appreciation.

"So, my dears, what brings you to the Wish Library this evening?" asked the Librarian. "It's late to be out in the woods."

"Didn't your wish computer tell you our wish?" asked Luca, pointing at the device.

Their Librarian was always using the computer to see where each wish was located and find out what people had wished for.

"Oh, that newfangled thing," said the Librarian. "I never did get the hang of modern technology."

Modern? thought Luca. The thing looked nearly as old as the redwood tree.

"We wish to know who is pranking us," said Raven.

"Interesting," said the Librarian. "What kind of

pranks have happened?"

"Lots of things," said Luca. "People's stuff was messed with, and someone let the chickens out of the coop. Twice. We were wondering if something magical was going on."

"Well, I *can* say that you two aren't the only visitors I've had this week," said the Librarian. "But I'm not really supposed to divulge other people's wishes. Confidentiality and all that."

"Someone else made a wish?" said Luca. "Who?"

The Librarian whispered in the owl's ear.

Luca and Raven raised their eyebrows at each other.

"Elsie agrees with me that as you are the famous Raven and Luca, and because you made a wish, we can make an exception to the rule this one time," said the Librarian. "Just don't tell HQ. Or Prudence. It was a camper named Jasper who found the Wish Library. He made the wish."

CHAPTER 6

Friend Forgotten

"Jasper?" asked Raven and Luca together. The name seemed familiar to them, but there was no one by that name in their camp.

"Oh. Oh dear," said the Librarian. "I was rather afraid this would happen."

"What?" asked Raven. "What happened?"

"Well, it seems that an unexpected consequence of Jasper's wish has caused you all to forget him," said the Librarian sadly.

Elsie covered her head with a wing.

"What was the wish?" asked Luca. He still couldn't remember there being anyone else in their group. But that did explain the sixth bed in his cabin.

"Jasper wished to disappear," said the Librarian. "And it seems that he's also disappeared from your memories."

"Do you know why he wanted to disappear?" asked Raven.

"Well, I'm afraid I have no idea," said the Librarian. "It's not my job to ask people why they want to make their wish, only to lend it to them."

"When is the wish due back?" asked Luca.

"Tomorrow morning at ten thirty a.m.," said the Librarian. "If it's not returned on time, Jasper will be forgotten forever!"

Raven and Luca still couldn't remember Jasper or what had happened to make him disappear. But they felt sure that no one would want to be forgotten forever. They had to make sure he returned the wish on time.

"Where's the exit?" asked Luca.

"Leaving so soon?" asked the Librarian. "I was hoping you'd have a cup of tea with me."

"Next time, I promise," said Raven. "We need to find Jasper."

"Of course," said the Librarian a little sadly. "I understand. The exit is right behind you."

A wooden door carved with the word EXIT appeared.

Raven and Luca thanked the Librarian and walked through the door. Immediately, they found themselves lying on the ground next to where the wishing well had been.

"We should get back before anyone notices we're missing," said Raven.

"And we need to figure out how to find Jasper," said Luca. "Maybe we can leave him a note on his bed?" Luca figured Jasper must be sleeping in his bed. Staying outside all night would be way too cold. And scary.

"Good idea!" said Raven.

At the farm, Austin was putting the last chicken back in the coop as Luca and Raven arrived.

"Where have you two been?" asked Austin as he shut the coop gate. "We had to do all the work!"

"We thought we saw a chicken headed into the forest," said Raven, thinking fast. "We went to catch it! But it was a raccoon."

Justin checked the coop gate and called the kids over to join him. "We're out of time for a campfire tonight," he said. "Everyone, go get showered and ready for bed."

Everyone groaned. But they were all tired after a busy day.

"I'll leave a note on the spare bed," Luca told Raven. "Hopefully Jasper will see it."

"What are you going to write?" asked Raven.

"I'll tell him we're friends and that we'll meet him at the wishing well at nine a.m.," said Luca. "That gives us plenty of time before the wish is due."

"Good idea!" said Raven. She hoped it would work.

CHAPTER 7

Flying Eggs

The next morning at breakfast, Luca told Raven that the note he'd left had vanished from the spare bed.

"I heard someone come into the cabin last night after everyone was in bed," said Luca. "I bet it was Jasper. This morning the blankets were all rumpled, so he definitely slept there. Hopefully he'll meet us at the Wish Library, like I asked him to."

"What are you talking about?" said Raven. She remembered they'd visited a Wish Library the day before but nothing about someone named Jasper.

"Oh no!" said Luca. "Did you forget?" He told her everything again. He wondered why he could remember what they'd learned from the Librarian about Jasper and his wish. *Maybe because I wrote the note,* he thought.

"How do we make sure we don't forget again?" asked Raven.

"Maybe we could write ourselves a note," said Luca, "since writing it down helped me remember before?"

"I have an idea," said Raven. She took a black marker from the art table at the back of the barn.

She rolled up her shirt sleeve and wrote "Jasper" on her arm. She handed the pen to Luca, and he did the same. Raven put the marker in her pocket.

Jasper

After Raven and Luca put their breakfast plates away, they checked the time: 8:50 a.m. That was just enough time to make it to the Wish Library entrance to meet Jasper.

But as they headed down the trail, Jess called out.

"Hey, you two need to do your chores before you can go anywhere!" Jess held out the egg collecting baskets. "You're on egg duty!"

"We need to hurry. Otherwise we'll miss Jasper," said Raven.

But with dozens of boxes to check in multiple hen houses, egg collecting was slow work. As Raven and Luca approached the last box, the lid opened in front of them. Two eggs drifted through the air.

"Jasper!" hissed Raven. "Is that you?"

The eggs hovered in place.

Luca seized his chance to speak before Jasper vanished again.

"Jasper, we know about the wish," said Luca. "We talked to the Librarian."

"We don't know why you wanted to disappear," said Raven. "But we can help you."

In the pigpen, Anna and Kiora were giggling and making oinking noises as they fed the pigs.

The eggs flew through the air. One hit Kiora, and the other hit Anna.

"Hey!" Kiora shouted. "Who did that?" Egg dripped down her shirt.

"It was them!" said Anna, pointing at Luca and Raven.

"It wasn't us!" said Luca. "It was…" But he stopped. No one remembered Jasper. And they couldn't tell anyone about the Wish Library.

Raven looked around to try to see where Jasper might have gone. "Jasper!" she said. No one answered.

The chicken coop gate opened by itself, but no one other than Raven and Luca noticed. And they were the only kids to notice footprints appearing as

Jasper ran away. The other campers were too busy laughing at Kiora and Anna as the eggs dripped down their clothes.

Jess and Justin hurried toward Raven and Luca. They looked angry.

———

"You two wait here," said Justin, pointing at some bales of straw outside the farm office. "We're going to have to call your parents about this."

But as Raven and Luca waited, a car pulled up. A man and a woman got out and walked to the office. A golden retriever on a leash followed behind them. The man knocked on the office door.

Jess opened it. "Can I help you?" she asked.

The woman said, "Yes, we're Jasper's parents. We were nearby, so we popped by to say hi."

"Jasper?" asked Jess, shaking her head. "We don't have a Jasper here this week."

"What do you mean?!" Jasper's mom said. She looked really worried.

Raven felt bad for her.

"We dropped him off on Monday morning. He's in cabin…" Jasper's dad trailed off. His forehead wrinkled, and he turned to his wife.

"I'm terribly sorry. I'm not actually sure why we're here," said Jasper's mom. "We were probably just out for a drive."

"No problem," said Jess.

"Poor Jasper!" said Luca. "His own parents have forgotten him!"

Raven imagined how she'd feel if her parents and Izzy forgot her. A tear dripped down her cheek.

Luca noticed Raven's tears and hugged her. "We'll find him and fix this!" he said.

Jasper's parents walked back to their car. But their dog started barking and pulling on its leash. It was trying to pull Jasper's dad toward the Barn Owl cabin.

"The dog still remembers Jasper!" Luca said to Raven, pointing at the barking dog. "Maybe wish magic doesn't work on animals?"

"What's gotten into you, Toby?" asked Jasper's mom.

The dog pulled and pulled. It broke free! The dog dashed toward the Barn Owl cabin.

"Stop!" yelled Jasper's dad, chasing after the dog. At the door to the cabin, the man grabbed the leash.

Toby kept barking and straining on his leash.

"Did you see a rabbit?" Jasper's dad said. "Silly boy!" He picked up the big dog, and the family got back into their car. The dog was still barking as they drove away.

Raven and Luca needed to find Jasper. And fast. If Jasper's own parents had forgotten him, they could be next.

Raven looked at her arm where she'd written Jasper's name. It was  starting to fade away. They had to make sure they didn't forget him too. She wrote over his name again with the marker.

"I bet he's in the cabin. That's where the dog wanted to go," said Raven. "Let's check it out."

Luca and Raven ducked down and ran behind the farm office so Jess and Justin didn't spot them.

In the Barn Owl cabin, Raven called out, "Jasper! If you're here, we can help you!"

Luca noticed that the top drawer next to Jasper's bed was half-open. He opened the drawer all the way and peered inside. There was an empty test tube labeled "Disappearing Wish." Jasper would need it to be able to return the wish to the Wish Library.

"Should we take it?" asked Raven.

Luca nodded. "We can give it to Jasper when we find him."

Raven looked at the clock in the cabin. "It's already 10:19. He's only got eleven minutes left!"

"Where should we look next?" said Luca.

"We could try the forest again," said Raven. "Jasper! If you can hear us, we're going to the Wish Library! Meet us there!"

CHAPTER 8

I Wish No More!

Raven and Luca poked their heads out the cabin door to see if Jess and Justin were around. Kiora and Anna were coming out of the Rabbits' cabin with clean clothes on. They looked upset.

"I wonder why Jasper threw the eggs at them," said Luca. He felt bad for the girls. But something stood out in his memory. Like Kiora and Anna had something to do with why Jasper had disappeared.

"I don't know," said Raven. "I think he must have had a good reason to vanish. I just hope we can find him."

Luca looked both ways for Jess and Justin. "I don't see anyone," he said. "Let's make a run for it!"

———

Outside the Wish Library, Luca and Raven called for Jasper. There was no answer.

"What time is it?" said Raven.

"Ten twenty-four!" said Luca.

"Jasper! We want to help you!" said Raven. "You need to return the wish!"

Suddenly a voice came from beside Raven. "I'm here," the voice said.

"Jasper!" said Luca. "We're so glad you came!"

"But I don't want to return the wish," said Jasper. "I want to stay invisible."

"Why?" asked Raven.

"Because everyone laughed at me," said Jasper. "And then I got my revenge by playing pranks. At first it felt good. But now I feel bad for throwing the eggs and getting you in trouble."

"Did Kiora and Anna do something to you?" asked Luca.

Jasper explained that Kiora and Anna had teased him when he'd fallen over in pig mud and then got covered in leaves and branches. He'd been so embarrassed he'd run into the woods. He'd said out loud "I wish I could disappear!" and the gold coin had appeared. When he'd spotted the wishing well, he'd decided to throw the coin in.

"I didn't know wishes could come true," Jasper continued. "And I guess I didn't think through what it would mean to disappear. I had no idea everyone would forget me—even my parents."

"Your dog remembers you though," said Raven. "And I bet he misses you."

Jasper sniffed. "I miss him too."

"Did the Librarian explain about the consequences?" said Luca.

"Kind of," said Jasper. "I signed a contract, but I didn't read all the small print."

"No one ever does," said Raven. "But if you don't

return the wish by ten thirty, you will be forgotten by everyone, forever!"

"You've only got two minutes left," said Luca. "No pressure, but um…you need to hurry!"

"I don't know," said Jasper. "I don't want to get in trouble!"

"We'll be by your side," said Raven.

"Yeah, we're your friends now," said Luca. "And friends stand up for each other."

"You did say you'd be my friend," said Jasper. "When we first met."

"I don't remember that," said Luca. "But it sounds like something I'd say."

"So what do you think?" said Raven. "Ready to return the wish so we can remember you?"

"Okay…so how *do* I return the wish?" Jasper asked.

"It's easy," said Luca. "Take the test tube and repeat three times, 'I wish no more.'"

Luca held out the test tube, and it floated in the air as Jasper picked it up.

"I wish no more, I wish no more, I wish no more!" Jasper said.

A swirling tornado of leaves surrounded the test tube. And slowly a boy appeared.

"Jasper!" said Raven. "I remember you now!"

"Me too! You brought chocolate chip cookies!" said Luca. He rubbed his belly, remembering the taste. "They were so good!"

"Luca! Focus!" said Raven. "Jasper, you need to drop the test tube in the wishing well!"

The well had just appeared, and an arrow with the words RETURN CHUTE glowed above it. Jasper dropped the test tube into the well and fell down after it.

Luca and Raven jumped in after him.

CHAPTER 9

Time for Tea

Jasper, Luca, and Raven slid down the wishing well slide and landed in a heap on the cushion.

"A return!" said the Librarian. "And so many visitors. How wonderful!"

"Did we make it in time?" Luca asked, looking around the Wish Library. There was no clock, but he was sure something was different about the Library compared to their last visit.

"Oh yes," said the Librarian. "I'm not much of a stickler for time, you know. A few minutes here or there doesn't matter to me."

Luca thought how different this librarian was from theirs in Lincoln. Their librarian was very strict about the rules.

"Would you like to make another wish?" the Librarian asked hopefully. "No one has asked for a pony recently. Or a baby sister. Oh, or a dragon. They're so much fun."

Raven shuddered. They definitely didn't want

to meet any magical creatures. "No, thank you," she said. "We need to get back to the camp before someone notices us missing."

"Can we stay a little longer?" said Jasper.

"Let's have tea!" said the Librarian. "Elsie, please return this wish to the shelf."

The owl took the test tube and flew up to one of the highest shelves in the Wish Library. The Librarian produced a teapot and some delicate cups, as if by magic, and laid them on a table with four chairs. She poured the tea.

"Come sit!" she said.

Raven and Luca shrugged. They supposed they were already in trouble for leaving the camp office. What could it matter if they were gone a little longer? Besides, Raven had promised they'd have tea on their next visit.

Raven sipped her tea. It was strawberry flavored and delicious.

"Has something changed since we were last here?" Luca said, looking around again. Everything felt a little cozier.

"Oh yes, we had a little growth spurt," said the Librarian. "This redwood grows faster than a regular tree. It's all the magic floating around in here, you see."

Luca could see now that the roots spread farther

than yesterday. The Librarian must have had to rearrange the shelves.

Raven looked at Jasper. He was staring into his teacup.

"What's wrong?" she asked.

"I don't feel ready to face everyone now that they'll remember what happened," said Jasper.

"If anyone teases you again," said Raven, "we'll stand up for you. We should have done that before."

"You were the only two who didn't laugh at me," said Jasper. "Thank you. That was why I didn't touch any of your things."

"I think it's time we got back," said Luca, putting down his teacup. "We can be by your side while you talk to the others."

⌒

"Raven, Luca, Jasper!" said Jess. Her hair was flying around her face as she ran toward them, and she looked worried. "Where have you all been?"

The three friends smiled with relief. Jess remembered Jasper!

"We just went for a walk," said Luca. "Sorry for any trouble."

"I was about to call your parents to tell them

about the egg throwing when I realized you had disappeared."

"So you didn't call them yet?" said Jasper.

"No, why?" said Jess.

"It was me who threw the eggs," said Jasper. "I'm really sorry. And I let the chickens out too."

"You need to find Kiora and Anna and apologize," said Jess. "And you can help me with chopping firewood while everyone else goes on a trail ride."

"We can help with the firewood too," said Luca, smiling at Jasper.

After chopping the firewood, Jasper, Raven, and Luca walked back to the animal pens. Jess said they could groom the goats again because they'd finished the chore so quickly by working together.

"I'm not looking forward to seeing the others," said Jasper. "I'll have to explain that it was me who threw the bear in the tree, put glue in the hairbrush, and poured slime on the glasses."

"Well, they shouldn't have all laughed at you," said Luca. Luca knew that playing pranks wasn't the way to deal with being teased. But he understood how Jasper had felt.

"No, but getting revenge didn't feel good like I thought it would," said Jasper. "And disappearing definitely didn't make things better in the end."

Raven looked over at the stables as the other

campers dismounted the horses. "They're back!" she said.

Jasper gulped as he turned to face the other campers.

"We'll be by your side," said Luca.

⌒

As the campers approached Jasper, Luca, and Raven, some of them laughed and held their noses, as if Jasper still smelled of pig mud.

"Hey!" said Luca. "That's not funny."

"Yeah!" said Raven. "Teasing people is mean."

"It's okay," Jasper said. "I was the one who played all the pranks. I was upset with how you all laughed at me, but I shouldn't have messed with your things, let the chickens out, or thrown the eggs."

Everyone stared at Jasper in silence.

He continued. "Pranking you all was the wrong thing to do. I'm sorry."

Anna gave Kiora a gentle nudge.

Kiora sighed. "I'm sorry for making everyone laugh at you," she said.

"Me too," said Anna.

The other campers joined in the apologizing. But Jasper held his hands up to stop everyone.

"No more sorries," he said. "We're here to have fun!" He paused and took a deep breath before finishing. "Oink, oink!" he said at last.

Everyone laughed. *With* Jasper this time.

That night, the campers gathered in the barn for their end-of-the-week dance. The barn was decorated with twinkly lights, and a disco ball turned slowly above the dance floor.

Justin wore a sparkly jacket and was choosing the music. "Our next song is dedicated to Raven and Luca, from Jasper," he said.

"Chicken Dance," came over the speakers, and Raven and Luca laughed.

The two took turns quacking, flapping, and shaking their butts in the middle of the dance floor. As they moved and sang, their cabinmates joined in.

Austin started doing a robot dance to the next song, which inspired the campers to all take turns doing their most embarrassing dance moves. Raven and Luca laughed and danced with their new friends.

The next morning, the campers made friend-
ship bracelets for each other. Jasper had cleverly
embroidered his name into his.

"So you never forget me!" he grinned.

Raven and Luca fastened the bracelets onto
their arms, where the black marker had almost
faded away.

Then, far too soon for the campers' liking, parents started arriving to collect their kids. Jasper
introduced his parents, and Toby, the golden
retriever, to Raven and Luca.

"I hear you were great friends to Jasper this
week," said Jasper's dad. "Thank you! If you're ever
up in Oregon, come visit us!"

"We'd love to!" said Raven.

Luca gave Toby a cuddle. He knew what pet he
would ask his mom for. A dog like Toby would be
perfect. Smart and loyal.

Their week at farm camp had ended, but they
would definitely ask their parents if they could
come back. And they couldn't wait to see their

Librarian and tell her how they'd met one of her colleagues.

"I wonder how many other Wish Libraries there are," Luca said as they waited for their parents to arrive. "We should ask next time we visit."

"It's funny to think about kids like us all over the world making wishes," said Raven. "I hope they don't have as many problems to fix as we do."

"Next time, we should wish for something just for fun," said Luca. "How about that flying wish at last? After all, what could go wrong?"